ANNE

ANNE

A Novel

Paal-Helge Haugen

Translated by Julia Johanne Tolo

Hanging Loose Press
Brooklyn, New York

www.hangingloosepress.com

Printed in the United States of America
10 9 8 7 6 5 4 3 2 1

Hanging Loose Press thanks the Literature Program of the New York State Council on the Arts for a grant in support of the publication of this book.

This book is the winner of the sixth annual Loose Translations Prize, jointly sponsored by Hanging Loose Press and the graduate writing program of Queens College, City University of New York. The competition is open to students and recent graduates of the MFA translation program.

Acknowledgments: Portions of this book first appeared in *Asympote Journal*, *Brooklyn Rail*, and *Copper Nickel Journal*.

Cover art by Eric Aho, Ice House (Night), 2016, Oil on linen, 16 x 20 inches (40.6 x 50.8 cm). Image courtesy of the artist and DC Moore Gallery, New York Artwork photography: Rachel Portesi.

Cover design by Marie Carter

Library of Congress Cataloging-in-Publication Data available on request

ISBN 978-1-934909-61-4

wrapped in orange flesh robes
William Burroughs

It's dark in here.

I see clearer now. Thin afternoon light slips in from a square
window high on the wall, a line across the cracked
floorboards. Soft quiver of dust there between light and darkness.
Hanging from the ceiling; large blankets of coarse wool. Dry tingling
in the tips of my fingers when I touch them.
Next to the door a brown uniform jacket with buttons turning green, I see
sleeves worn thin, full of darker spots.

Smell of leather and worn clothes as I walk across the floor. Human clothing.
Against the wall a small brown-painted chest. When the lid swings in towards
the wall, fine rust sprinkles from the hinges. Uneven letters
have been carved with a knife underneath the lid.
Dreng Salmondsen. Almost unreadable in the half darkness. Underneath linen
shirts and bolts of dark cloth there's a small cardboard box. The lid is smooth and
white, the bottom is red. A weak sweet smell when the lid comes off, almost
nothing. I turn, into the line of light.

Two pieces of paper from a calendar
Twelfth of May Fifth of October
Small comb of lusterless metal
Blue embroidered letters on linen fabric: Jesus
Brown photograph of a woman with a big mouth
For Anne from Hege
Spoon with dark lines

When I walk down the steep stairway, mild air on my skin. A weak sound
escapes the wood with each step.
Out there eyes are being filled with pale sun. I lean against the wall, and feel
blood pulsing in my palms. My blood, an even weak rhythm.

March, snow is wet.
Light is all around the grey corners of the house.

I

The long white-painted house has one door only,
a dark open square.
It's early in the morning, and quiet.
Outside two tall men in black clothing,
clear against the white snow.

E. DE

GENDER: FEMALE

N.	Death date	Time of funeral	interment	The deceased's full Name and Civil Status (Profession) Added for Adults whether he (she) was unmarried, married, Widower (Widow) or divorced
32	25 - 1	30 - 1	30 - 5	Gunhild Knutsdtr. Nese, Married

Birthplace and for conscript Men added: Time and Place of confirmation	Residence	Given Cause of Death
Holen	Berg	Bleeding during Parturition

AD

If Married Women: Husband's, if Child: Father's Name and Civil Status	Birth Year (Month Day for Children up to 5 Years and Conscript Men)
Daniel Torsen Nese, Farmer	1872

Was Doctor called during Deceased's last Disease	Has the Death been reported by Them to the Probate Court	Remarks
Yes, but was late	Yes	

In the drifting winter all the houses have closed
doors. Their brown walls are low, and inside in half-
darkness animals are turning heavily.
A leaf-thin moon shows itself early,
naked behind thin air.
At night the floor is cold underneath my feet.
Every night sleep with blank inconceivable dreams.
Every morning drown in cold and white.

Little children walk with short steps in the snow. They hear
the trees twitching, and stand still for a long time.
Sometimes women in blue come onto deserted
roads. They speak low to each other, and breathe white fog
from their mouths.

In May the evening shows itself light and unmoving. A shiny hub of frost lies in the quiet air underneath pine trees and down in stone cellars in empty houses. You can walk over the yellow mire, over wet moss where your footprints become holes filled with brown water.
You can walk for a long time before the dark comes, walk home with tired feet and fall into heavy sleep.

In May in the evening I see birds with large wings disappear into the forest. Long still they scream in there, before everything alive falls silent. When it's dark three hares come out in the clearing by the edge of the forest. They sit in the short grass,
lift their heads and listen.

after rain black stones
the snail, soft under green leaves
feels the wetness

Under ferns: cool air against my face.
Earth is blacker than out there, and shiny
stag beetles crawl under dead straws.
My knees press round holes into wet earth,
cool earth.
When I lay my ear to the ground, mumbling
voices down there.

In here it's green and wet.

From the bed I see the moon through uneven
glass panes.
Moon with unmoving face.
Shiny matte
and a thin ring around it.
The wind has gone quiet in the trees, in the tall lark,
in low bushes by the stone fence.
Someplace in the darkness are red berries under
moist leaves.

I think of meager men and pale children.

The boat glides out from land, out from the river bank where heather grows high. In hazy air a young man poles his boat over shiny water. Headlands lie in shadow, water is silver.

Beyond the cape he stands still in the boat, the piece of string from his hands a matte stripe.

There man and boat are almost one with water and light, translucent and trembling with big holes of silver.

As he gets close to the other side, he disappears from my eyes.

Smooth fish between cold rocks
A black back, then gone

Rain in my face
Out there light roads in water

Tracks from his boots in the watery earth. Father. Daniel. His hands
in the field all day, when he comes home his voice is coarse and slow.
I look in his eyes and know they look like mine. I recognize his movements.
Every time he bends down, every time he lifts the cup to his mouth.
Late at night, when I walk through the room where he sleeps, I hear
his breath in the darkness.

The smell of grass that falls under the scythe,
and a light cloud of yellow dust with each
stroke. Men in a line, in white
shirts and pants of homespun black wool.
They move evenly forwards, with
long, round movements singing in their bodies.
Underneath wide hats faces I know.
When I lie on my back in the grass,
heat collects and overpowers.

Hege, sister, thin in a blue dress, stands
on the hill and calls:
Anne, come

His hands are uneasy when he speaks. Those old hands. His eyes
have sunk further in, become more narrow. He doesn't look at me. I see a blue
filled vein in his thin neck.
His lips are moving slowly. Coarse and heavy words.
Talk about these people. Say names. Living names
of dead people.

Pers-Margit.

In the evening a small crooked woman behind the house. Black hair
long against her yellow flesh.
Pers-Margit who didn't get any food from Aslaug Viki.
Spit twice in the yard. In the summer two small boys drowned in Viki.
Pers-Margit who wasn't allowed to die before they cut her tongue off.
It was winter, and she wasn't allowed to die.

In autumn a thin man stands on the bridge, in high boots and a broad overcoat.
I recognize his back when I walk past in fog and rain, when it's
late.
Aslak. His hands hard on the railing. I walk faster, cold
river breath against my knees, blowing against my dress.
The red plaid dress.
Under the bridge the water drags slow and dark. A sound you bring home,
and into sleep.

Aslak quiet. He stands there on the slippery boards for a long time.
I know what is said when everyone speaks quietly, know about the mute woman
who went into the river one autumn afternoon.
A patched shawl between rounded rocks.
Nothing.
Little children with inflated stomachs and big eyes, like ash.
Black hunger. Hell.

He's standing in the same spot, a whisper reaching low
over cold water :
Sigrid

Evening grows out of bushes and stone fences, down
over hills and plains.
Your shoes get wet when you walk in the grass.
Children walk home and call out to each other between
houses. Their voices are loud and clear, they carry
far out.
The horse goes down to the water, dark, bends its head
and drinks.

FIRST SCHOOL LEVEL. PREPARATION FOR READING PRACTICE.
SECOND ROW. TWO SYLLABLE WORDS.
11. SOMETHING ABOUT MYSELF. I am but a Child; but with Time
I might still grow up. I possess both Body and Soul. The former I can
see with my Eyes and touch and feel with my Hands, but my Soul
I can neither see nor touch. My Body consists of four Parts: Head,
Chest, Belly and Limbs. Each of these Parts consists of Skin, Flesh,
Bone and Blood. I also have Hair and Nails. That each Part serves its Purpose,
I know for certain, but I do not know yet, what Purpose each Part will serve.
This I shall know in Time.

On top of the hill
Two men under low clouds
Clear faces in the wind, clear eyes
And a thin flute, the sound over dry forest earth
Breath against silver

Run fast over bridges, feel the wood sing with each step.
Rain is far away. By the cherry tree brown bees float with a low
trembling sound. When I look up in strong light, houses are pale up there
in the hills, they dissolve in sun. Thin shadow houses with walls like waves
in the heat over the fields. Houses I can't recognize.

The dogs lie still in the new grass, with eyes closed.
Shirts of white linen hang in the wind,
and an old man walks across the muddy yard.
The day against my eyes.

Smell of heavy dust from the big book. The brown leather
feels like horns. Pages with dark stains.
Marks from fingers, my fingers, other fingers.
Letters pressed deep into the paper,
like squatting insects, still insects with open claws.
Isaiah.
Taste of dark water. Lead and dead birds.

I have tested Thee in the Furnace of Affliction

In measure, when it shooteth forth,
Thou wilt debate with it: he stayeth his rough Wind
in the Day of the East Wind

In the bay four boys with naked backs
and black pants, crouching in the sand.
I see a white body in the water. His arms,
his hips in green water, gliding
like a slender fish out there.
The water ripples from a sudden wind.
Their voices reach me.

Lord, all Wisdom and Nowlege is in You, You now the Past All that has happen and that is happenin, You observe, and what is comin is revealed to Your eyes, Lord You now how our Days are number and by You is decided what our mision in life should be. You observ the Joy and Sorow, the Sucess and Aversity that by Your Will shall meet us. O. Father, we now not what will happen to us; but You now and in Your Hand we are safe, be with us and have Your Son pray for us, so nothin may hurt us. Your Sprit shine the light on us and with our Sprits we are Yours so that the dark itself become light to us, and so that nothin may separate us from Gods Love, Christ Jesu our Lord

Five in the morning. It's getting light outside.
Still all sounds are indistinct and distant, behind a film of wax. I feel
warmth from my own body, feel the heaviness in me. Human.
A warm body.
Sometimes I think there's a spiral twisting deep into the earth, without
restraint, almost unnoticeably it twists around. Twists me around, when I lie
on my back with my eyes closed.

When I sit halfway up, I look out into grey
morning. Out there the gate is open in the drizzle.
It's getting light. The clock shows five, and I can't sleep.

Blood streams down on thick hardwood boards, out from the open
sheep's stomach. Blood on white wool. Red steaming stomach,
white smooth membrane over all that meat. Meat
meat. Food for humans, for me. Red warm. Hide me
The sheep's eyes twitch long after the strike, flies are crawling over the
inversed eyeball, they sew themselves to it, they live.
Tongue out between short teeth. Legs strangely strained and stiff.
Torjus has warm wet hands, thin blood–water streams down and
blends with the mud around his boots.
I stand there and feel my body warm in the wind,
my pulse beating in my temples.
They lead the last sheep out.

Thou shall not covet thy neighbor's wife or his manservant
or his maidservant or his ox or his ass or anything that is
thy neighbor's
That is
We shall fear and love God so we do not lure or threaten from our neighbor his
wife servants or oxen but help so that wife and servants stay with him and give
what they owe
266 Is there a just man upon earth that does good and sins not
No
271 Is then all lust and yearning evil
There is in the soul an innocent urge to satisfy the needs of the body like the
desire for food drink sleep movement and so on
This desire was in man in his innocence and therefore is not sinful

272 But are there not many sins that follow these natural desires
Certainly
This is caused by nature's deep depravity which is a part of all things and
which makes the desires of the innocent sinful and impure if we do not
diligently fight against it
273 What are the sinful things that especially awaken sinful desires
These are
1 Excess lavish and lascivious things
2 Foreign things

Sunday afternoon.
Hymns that taste of calcite and white altar table cloths.
Afterwards empty for a long time. Walk around with bare
feet, in a room of wide organ pipes and
vibrating old voices.

The weather vane is pointing north, unmoving.

The clock on the wall continues with even dry snaps.
On the table a black long insect,
round and round in little circles.

Walk on roads when the shingle is grey and wet.
Swallows dipping down from the sky,
low over wet fields.
Look at my own hands. See small muscles
move there, and hair like down against the light.
Can't stand those hands. They're a little big,
and mine.

Down below the hills a man is plowing in the rain.
Johannes.

On the white painted wall the image of his suffering.
The cross, strangely shining and beautiful. A smooth tree without branches,
above thunderclouds are hanging low.
His neck is deeply bent, that neck with young frizzy hair. I can't
see the face. Red drops are dripping under the thorns.
Free us. Free us. Shatter all shiny weapons. Give the men clean hands.
Many children are not yet born. Thunderclouds hang low, almost black.

This is my Body. Four nails through the feet,
pounded in between bare tendons. Blood in purple stripes,
dried against the thin side of the upper body.

I'm thirsting

By the foot of the cross a woman with eyes transfixed,
one arm reaching out with the hand open.
Maria. Maria. I know you can't see him.
I know you feel the nails in your flesh.
In the evening light his naked chest shines yellow.
Behind the split curtain a mumbling
of rusty knives.

Four Books about true Christianity authored by
Dr. Johan Arndt
died as General-Superintendent in Zelle 1621

a new Stone and in the Stone a new Name written, which no man
knoweth, saving he, that receiveth it

Outside: dense darkness.

Christmas night is long. In the loft everyone is sleeping now, on new bundles of hay, under old blankets. Down here the candle burns slant, flares up every now and then, falls back down in a low blue flame. Christmas night is long and dark. You can see the one you will wed. See him in the mirror when you are alone.

Walk three times around the table. Candle burns more quiet. Words that old women remember and speak with low voices, or hide behind unmoving eyes.

Friend sits on the tuft
and stirs the good earth
In Christ's name, step forth
and three God's angels in God's word

The uneven surface is spotty and matte. I move
the light over. I stand here. All shadows sharpen
their edges.
Whiteness collects, moves over the bottom
of the mirror. Can I see my own mouth? Closer now.

A red stripe runs slowly down the glass.
In there pale eyes

II

The wind moves through days, nights.
Wind and light in the maple tree when I awake.
Dark wind for supper.
Float sleeping on streams of wind over a wide night.
Shiny translucent skin under my eyes in the mirror,
dry skin with little cracks in my palms.
Little boys stand on hilltops and feel the wind
breathe, feel it lifting wide shirts. They tread easily,
with long steps, and roll around in the grass.

When I open the door, wind against my face,
I walk with short quick breaths. Down on the plains
I have to bend forward and button my wool jacket
high on my throat.

Man that is born of a Woman is of few days and full of Trouble. He cometh forth like a Flower, and is cut down, he fleeth also as a Shadow, and continueth not. Thou puttest my Feet also in the Stocks, and Lookest narrowly unto all my Paths; thou settest a Print upon the heels of my Feet. And he, as a rotten Thing, consumeth, as a Garment that is Moth-Eaten.

Job. Lean shadow. I sat by your side in the ashes, but you didn't see me.

I walk over the marsh, little bubbles escape the mud between
patches of moss. Down there short light-red plants. Juicy stems and threads
with rows of sticky drops, clear in the light, they stick to the skin when
you touch them. If you bend down, you see flies stuck there.
Dry shells of flies. Brown water into my shoes now.
My hair frizzes in the humid air.

Slide through the landscape, slide in behind the walls, tired.
The days are tightening around my body.
Hollow days of lye, of ash.

Something that grows big in the body, and leaves behind unease, empty. I can wake in the night and know, without words. What will happen. Carry it hidden underneath the skin. Pulse beats so quickly, breathing short, changed. Something is being twisted around in there, something is being screwed tight. I want to go out, fasten new days to my chest.

A dry cough is tearing at my chest, chasing black dots in front of my eyes.
Every so often I have to sit and rest my forehead in my hands.
Afterwards breaths like long knives in there.
Sometimes I walk out under the maple when it starts.
Sometimes I lie down flat in the grass.
Sometimes I taste salt in my mouth.

Windows are open, day and night. Sometimes gusts of wind from outside reach all the way into the bed, mostly in the evening. Evening, when the house is quiet, and I can touch the darkness.

The significant *source of infection* in the infectious diseases is the *recently excreted* fluids from the sick organs. In that sense the most dangerous element of *pulmonary tuberculosis* is the sputum. How long the bacterial infections survive in these excretions differs greatly. Most will die quickly with desiccation, high temperatures and sunlight. They will usually live the longest in cold, moist air and darkness.

Further it is important to consider the diseased or the carrier of the infection's contaminated *hands, towels, handkerchiefs, bandages, bed clothes* and *daywear,* also *eating* and *drinking utensils, books, toys, house air,* and different *bodily discharges* can transfer the disease. From these sources the infection is transferred by *touch* (kiss, handshake), by enjoyment of *water* and *foodstuffs,* by *inhalation,* and by *stinging insects.*

Deep hollow areas between tendons on top of my hand. Every day deeper, a little deeper. Skin tight over hips, bones protrude clearly, hard and pointed. When the cough tears, I think the bones are coming out, digging their way through a membrane of skin, I put my hands over my chest and hold on. Close my eyes and hold, as I'm coughing up something with foaming light-red stripes. Coming from down there. From me.

The night brings burning cheeks, drives a great unrest through the body, long stakes of fire and ice, holding me to the bed and burning me. Every night. Icefrost in the fire. My eyelids close.

When the infectious agent has gotten into the lungs, gray white clots the size of hemp seeds are formed in the lung tissue. A sticky yellow fluid is created in the air sacs; containing rejected cells from the walls of the air sacs and white blood cells. The number of clots increases, and after a while the clots merge into bigger masses. The central parts of these masses die out after a while, the texture becoming looser, like cheese, and lastly cavities of different sizes form inside the clots. Often there are also calciferous deposits. The cavities have smooth capsule-clad walls. During this development, several veins will typically break. If these are smaller veins, the patient's sputum will have light-red stripes or spots.

They say I have to leave. They turn away, and say I will be
well. They say rest, clear, pure air, sunshine, white beds, help, medicine,
invigorating baths.
They say it will be good. Soon.
They pack clothing in a box, they come to get me, keep me steady, help me
into the carriage. They drive me off. Early morning, they stand there
and watch me leave.
April morning. I let my head fall back
and hold on tight to the seat. I'm going away.

The building lies on top of a slight hill. Long white-painted house. Sanatorium. On the road in the park two women are walking, arm in arm. Wide capes of grey wool hang loosely about their shoulders. They turn, look, speak together. The weather is grey and mild. We walk through the gate. Rough gravel beneath our steps. People dressed in white receive us, help with cool hands.

The room is white and oblong. High up on one of the shorter walls is a window with four glass panes, in the window sill is a houseplant, low and luxuriant. The cup-shaped flowers have a strong red color.

The bed is against the wall, it's a bed made of black-painted iron rods, here and there the paint is worn and there is the lusterless shine of metal. Under the window is a mirror, a round table and a shelf of brown wood, on it is an enameled water pitcher. On the floor a cup with a shiny lid of metal and wet sawdust inside. Over the bed a small reproduction on cheap paper, it shows Christ on the cross, only the head with the crown of thorns and a part of the naked chest. At the bottom in Gothic letters *O the Head so cursed*.

The frame is narrow and golden.

On the wall by the bed greasy spots from heads that have rested against the white limestone.

Spots from many women's hair, women no one remembers clearly anymore. Women who have gone away, to other places, other rooms.

Over fruit trees in the garden I see three low houses, on the other side of the river. Three houses through sunshine and heavy heat. Pale, they are frail images, perhaps I can erase them with my hand, if I want. I know: one could walk across the river, one could come close, see the houses are there, place hands on split wood, push palms against and feel: Fixed. Hard. One could smell Sun Wood Tar, I know.

They are pale houses, through warm air. On the gravel road a man walks, white shirt and a dark coat, placed over his arm.

The young woman seems tired and worn out, she is tall and rather skinny. Cheeks shine brightly red in her pale face, skin is dry and warm, almost translucent. Sweat breaks out on her forehead, especially during the intense cough contractions that come every few minutes. Often loose foaming sputum will follow. Eyes are shining. Pulse is fast. Voice is a little hoarse, otherwise unremarkable. Hair is dull and lifeless. Breathing is a bit short, and seems strained. She sits in the same position, doesn't move much. Her hands are in her lap, one gets the impression that she is looking at a specific point on the wall, close to the floor.

Every morning get up from bed. Walk across the floor to the table, to the mirror. Six steps forward. This is important. Six steps.
Smell of lye when I lift the soap. Pitcher of water, little bubbles of air against its inside.
Feel face wet, skin trembling against water, some enter the mouth. The pitcher has been standing here in the night while I was sleeping, water is lukewarm.
Hair is straight and dull now. A crackling sound under the comb when I sort it out. Don't look into the mirror much, don't see the face too clearly.
I know anyway.
Cling tight to this morning, hold on.

THE FOLLOWING MEDICATIONS MAY BE USED
IN THE TREATMENT OF THE PATIENT:
With high fever Antipyrine 0.50
With strong nightly sweats Camphoric Drops 1.0
With troublesome and persistent cough Dovers powder 0.10
The patient shall also daily take Sirolen 10 pct
Solution and Orexin-tbl. 4 pcs to counteract
lack of appetite and feelings of bodily inadequacy

Footprints from people walking under tall trees. Dogs
can be heard far away.

Clear translucent winter
underneath my fingers.

Tired, unquenchable, taut across a blanket of warm wool. Jitter like
heavy fire back and forth through my body, burns me dry.
The tall clock ticks, drives pieces of metal into unmoving
arms, leaves sharp grains of marble under my eyelids.
Weight of my head against soft down, soon everything must tear. Fall
soon. Streams of hot milk in my limbs, heavier than sea and mountain.

Sleep, through a dense winter, wake up on the other side, open my eyes
and walk out warm into melting snow.

OUR BODY HE SHALL GIVE US
BACK WITH SKIN AND HAIR
AS IF WE WERE ALIVE
AWAKE AND AWARE

The light burns down, heavy drops fall:
Stairs of tallow. Skin wet, inside linen.
Words like gravel against my tongue. O Thy Wounds So Deep

A horse came here, with short halting steps.
A brown horse with light hooves.
Taut, push my feet against the bottom of the bed. The light
burns down, and a Hart panteth after Water.

Innermost in the white room,
with hands outstretched:

Suddenly this emptiness
Searching with fingers along the edge
of darkness
Searching with fingers along the edge
of vision
Fingers sink
I turn inwards and look

Late, when the shell around my body
has loosened
Who's breathing on me

When I lie completely still: Hard heartbeats
in the closet. Soft holes in the floorboards
in front of the bed. Breaking through. Roses of
blood and cast iron. Dark smell of meat,
sex
Snails over my nails
Horse's sweat, blue roads under belly
Wet mirrors
Graveyard song   Pale Sun
My ship is filled with hands
The snake is creeping through an eye of steel and Christ
is in the garden, wearing maple

Her forehead is cold and wet. She lies with her eyes closed, opens them sometimes, and then immediately closes them. Shiny eyes. Sharp twitches through her body, you see muscles underneath thin skin, see them stay taut a while, and quiver. Breathing is shorter now, and heavier, interrupted by coughs. Coughs that drive blood out to the edges of her mouth. She is given half a glass of water in which half a teaspoon of kitchen salt has been dissolved, then ice-cold milk, spoon by spoon.

The moon has large spots of fungus and mold
Heat heat throw me into the sea   Write Thy name
Jesus on my heart under earth and stone earth
and stone
Long dorms of wind-swept children
Metal-wind   Smell of animals
Sand scatters under my skin   Hege naked in the woods
                                    Hands mouths
Judas pierces with needles living
Blind kittens looking for udders for big
troughs of cascading rain
Fire-tongues
in
the mirror   Tight shoals of bayonets through my eyes

At dusk the owl sits on the fence, moves
with little jumps on the stones and shakes its wings. Sits
still then and cries.

dress white   carry out

. . . . Warm holes in the stone wall . . . . Horselights . . . . Dead
men in red hats . . . . Summer-rain . . . . Winter
organ . . . . O MY SOUL IT WANDERS . . . . Bleeding
from the butter . . . . Fiddles with twisted necks . . . .
Lazarus without peace . . . . in the wilderness . . . . AMONG THE
MANY THINGS OF THIS WORLD . . . .
Face will soon form big cracks
Little men with drums and whistles
are moving now

insect–streams

frost

earth: speech : wings

She squeezes her hands hard around the edge of the bed, without opening her eyes. Let's go and falls back on the pillow, turns her head towards the wall. The pillowcase is moist around her throat and head. Pulse is fast and uneven. Her breaths can be heard clearly in the room, rough and hard. Her nose has become more pronounced, it points out from under her thin skin. Lips seem dryer, and her cheeks have hollowed, all the lines in her face are clear, deep tracks. The beats of her pulse are getting weaker now, a distant shaking under the skin.

needle now
under stab here
lord under deep here
you u

Into the empty room enters a woman of about fifty years, small and with a slight curve to her back. She is dressed in a long white gown and has a kerchief over her hair.

Bed and chair are moved into the middle of the floor, closet doors are opened, the picture of the crucified taken down and put on the table. A lighter square is left on the yellowed wall.

Windows are firmly closed and the keyhole is stuffed with cotton.

The room is warm, there are still embers in the oven. In the middle of the floor a large tub of cold water is placed and in it a smaller bucket.

Into the bucket she pours permanganate, formalin and boiling water.

The woman stirs with a wooden spoon, and the formalin-steam starts to rise densely from the roaring water.

She hurries out of the room and closes the door tight after her. The room soon fills with formalin-steam.

After 7-8 hours she comes in with a wet kerchief over her mouth and opens doors and windows. Outside a sharp wind, it's cold.

The next day the room is washed with concentrated green soap water, with ammonium chloride added to remove the bad smell that has set in the walls. It smells like wet wood for a long time, clean wood and green-soap.

Windows stay open a few more days, in strong eastern wind.

They carry her out. In a long wooden case. Weight of a body,
pressure against the hands of the six men that carry it. Gently out through
the door, the narrow door. Outside there's cold sunshine, clear, sharp.
Downways from the house are human figures, close together. Horse and
sled wait by the road, the horse with a layer of frost on its side. Thin snow
over the naked, frozen earth, ridges stand out like ribs, worn-off,
wind-grinded. Human voices against the cold house walls, a hymn, meeting
the six men and their bare heads.
They carry her out, across the courtyard.

O MORTAL SEE MY COUNTENANCE
I WAS ALIVE LIKE THEE
AND WALKED THE EARTH LIKE ANY MAN
WHAT I AM YOU SHALL BE

They burn clothes behind the outhouse. A red plaid dress, a blue heavy woolen skirt, long yellowed stockings of wool, a gray homespun coat with silver patterns on the edges, shirts, a rose-painted kerchief. It's difficult to make them burn.

Included in this novel are some older texts, taken from the following sources: Landstad's Book of Hymns, The Bible (Job's Book, Isaiah the Prophet) Erik Pontoppidan's Explanation of Dr. Martin Luther's Small Catechism, Johan Arndt's True Christianity, Illustrated Medical Handbook for Use in the Home by V. Ucherman, and P.A. Jensen's Textbook for Elementary School. I have also used formulations from church books, and a prayer of unknown origin, found on the title page of a Bible.

P-H. H

Translator's Note

It is my honor to introduce to English-speaking readers what may just be Paal-Helge Haugen's most singular work. As you will read in his biography, Haugen has had other works translated into English, and *Anne* has been translated into several languages, but this is the first time the book is available in English. This is curious considering it's never been out of print in Norway, where it was first published in 1968. *Anne* made her way into my own family almost 40 years ago when a good friend of my parents gave the book to my mother. Although she read a lot of fiction she was less familiar with poetry and found *Anne* to be perfect because it read like a novel in verse. The book stayed on our shelf until it found a new reader in me some 30 years later.

When I first took *Anne* off the bookshelf, I found it to be a strange, dark book, with an obscured woman's profile on the cover; also it was made from an unusual material, a thick paper that almost felt like cloth (this was Det Norske Samlaget's fantastic first edition of the book). The small, square book did not seem to me any less strange as I started to leaf through it, only to reveal sparse and rectangular pieces of text on each page, making me wonder what kind of literature this could be. The book was literally a precious object that defied definition. I read it several times in that first sitting, working to make sense of the way narrative emerges, the play between the found text and Paal-Helge Haugen's own words.

Det Norske Samlaget's current description of *Anne* reads as follow:

> *Anne* by Paal-Helge Haugen was first published in Norway in 1968, and was soon considered a modern classic. The book introduced the genre *punktroman,* and has had an important legacy in Scandinavia. Documentary fragments from sources such as Bible verses, hymns, medical and death records, are woven together with personal narrative in this intense story of a young woman's life and death in rural Norway around the turn of the 20th century. (Italics added)

I think the term *punktroman* holds the key to the magic of this book. Initially I thought this should be translated as *bullet-pointed novel,* as *punkt* in Norwegian means *point* and *roman* means *novel.* To me, the term invokes the idea of building blocks, meant for the reader to arrange as she sees fit. Later on I read another interesting translation of *punktroman* in Karl Ove Knausgård's *My Struggle 5,* which was *pointillist novel.* This translation refers to the technique of painting in which small, distinct dots of color are applied in patterns to form an image, made famous by Georges Seurat.

The pointillist painting technique relies on the ability of the eye and mind of the viewer to blend the color spots into a fuller range of tones, and I can see how this feels analogous to *punktroman.* Implicit in the idea of *punktroman* is that what the reader brings to a work like *Anne* is as important to the production of meaning as what she has been given by the author of the book. When you look at a pointillist painting from the right distance, the eye fills in the "missing information"; similarly, a reader of *Anne* will bring her experience and understanding to the book and make meaning of the fragments Haugen has included.

The closer you look at a pointillist painting, however, the fewer shapes your eyes are able to make out. When you are standing right in front of one of these works, your eyes only perceive dots and the meaning dissolves. In *Anne,* Haugen has arguably provided the outline of a novel, so that one book contains the possibility for different versions, and allows room for the reader's imagination. However, Haugen's story does not dissolve upon closer inspection, but rather it gains significance, begs for interpretation. The details included – the placement of found text within the work, the way in which the narrative plays out – all contain a wealth of information to unfold.

I began my translation in the fall of 2014, and although the similar sentence structure of Norwegian and English allowed for much of the work to move smoothly from one language to the other, I also met with challenges. The most significant one was how to represent the different tones in *Anne,* which to me are very much impacted by the two languages used, and the cultural significance of this.

To explain, much of the found text in *Anne* is written in Riksmål (or Rigsmaal as it was called back then), as most religious and public texts from the 19th century were in Norway. Riksmål can be explained as Danish with only minor Norwegian modifications. Until 1814, Norway was a part of Denmark. After several hundred years of living with Danish language and culture, it became increasingly important to celebrate Norwegian history and culture, which led to a change in our written language. Language reforms (the first in 1907) have contributed to Riksmål becoming more "Norwegianized" and since 1929 the form was renamed Bokmål. Of

Norway's two official written languages, Bokmål is now the more common.

Haugen's own words in *Anne* are written in Nynorsk (originally Landsmål), a language that was created by collecting words from different dialects around Norway, to create a written tradition closer to how people actually spoke in the country. Nynorsk is today the other official written language in Norway, but there is public debate about whether we should continue to use it and teach it in schools. Det Norske Samlaget exclusively publishes books in Nynorsk, which is one of the ways that this beautiful language is being kept alive.

The nuances between Riksmål and Bokmål and the contrast of Riksmål to Nynorsk are clear to a native Norwegian speaker, who would know the story of Norway's written languages. Norwegians would recognize that the found text in *Anne* is dated from the use of Riksmål, specifically from differences such as the Danish *aa* being used instead of *å*, or the soft Danish consonants of *b, d* and *g* in place of the harder consonants *p, t* and *k*, which are used in modern Bokmål.

From a translator's standpoint, I was concerned about what the text would lose in English. In the religious texts this was less of an issue, as I could look to the King James Bible for language that reads as dated to English-speaking readers in a similar way to how Riksmål reads to a Norwegian speaker. In other cases, I would try to be historically accurate by looking up synonyms and choosing one that was commonly used in the 19th century.

As I started to fine-tune my translation, I tried another method that I think brought a lot to the book. Because I couldn't reproduce the languages and history of Norway in my English translation, I looked at phrases that would be jarring to a Norwegian reader, and tried to produce a similar effect in English. In this endeavor, Paal-Helge Haugen came to my rescue many times and offered solutions that heightened the English translation. Haugen also generously helped me work through dialect words and meanings that I had not perceived, as I myself write in Bokmål, not Nynorsk.

After this process, as I reread the English translation side-by-side with the Norwegian, the strangeness I was perceiving in the Norwegian was beginning to come through in the English, even in the places where I was worried the different languages of the original were the only possible sources of the unfamiliar tone. I think John Berger's thoughts on the triangularity of translation are fitting here:

Translation is not a binary affair between two languages but a triangular affair. The third point of the triangle being what lay behind the words of the original text before it was written. True translation demands a return to the pre-verbal. One reads and rereads the words of the original text in order to penetrate through them to reach, to touch, the vision or experience that prompted them. One then gathers up what one has found there and takes this quivering almost wordless "thing" and places it behind the language it needs to be translated into. And now the principal task is to persuade the host language to take in and welcome the "thing" that is waiting to be articulated.

I've often thought about how Haugen began this project, about what first piqued his interest. I've purposely not asked him because I think a novel like *Anne* likes to pose more questions than it answers. A lot is gained from allowing the readers to make up their own ideas of how this book came into being. Personally, I like to think that Haugen came across the source text that is used in *Anne* and found that a narrative was emerging: inviting him to share the story that he was seeing.

What was most important for me to show in my translation was the care with which Haugen has used found text in *Anne*, at once allowing the narrative to be impacted by and to impact this text, but also, very carefully not allowing the book to be read in a single way. This can be seen in Haugen's approach to assembling the book, as I pointed out earlier, from the way the found text is placed throughout the book – be it medical reports, death records, incantations, or Bible verses – to the fact that even in his note on the sources used for *Anne*, he does not specify which text is used on what page. Curious readers might task themselves with figuring out what has been used where, while a more intuitive reader might enjoy not knowing for sure. The room for play, and for the making of many different meanings, is the greatest gift I think Haugen gives his readers. This may be the "quivering, wordless thing" hiding behind the (many) language(s) in *Anne*, and what I hope English-speaking readers will enjoy most about this very special book.